THE CITY OF RAINBOWS

Library of Congress Cataloging-in-Publication Data

Foster, Karen Sharp.
       The city of rainbows : a tale from ancient Sumer / retold and
illustrated by Karen Foster.
       p. cm.
       The sage and benevolent King Mer-kar, who ruled Uruk in
Mesopotamia about 2700 B.C. and who was a royal ancestor of Gilgamesh,
triumphs over the foolish King Sukesh-danna of Aratta.
       ISBN 0-92-417170-7
       [1. Folklore—Iraq.] I. Title.
PZ8.1.F8146 Ci 1999
398.2′09567′02—dc21   99-6458
                                                                  CIP

Copyright 1999
The University Museum
University of Pennsylvania
Philadelphia

THE CITY OF RAINBOWS

RETOLD AND ILLUSTRATED
BY
KAREN FOSTER

Once, a very long time ago, King Mer-kar ruled over the city of Uruk in ancient Sumer. Around the walls of Uruk lay rich orchards, fields, and gardens. Inside the gates, there were fine houses and shops selling treasures from the four corners of the world.

Overlooking the whole city was the temple of the great goddess Inanna. Its walls were made of bricks painted in gemstone colors and polished so they gleamed in the sunlight. People called Uruk the City of Rainbows.

Tales of Uruk's wonders traveled far and wide, until one day word reached the city of Aratta, beyond the eastern mountains. The trader told the baker; the baker told the potter; and soon everyone had stopped what they were doing to hear of the splendors of Uruk.

King Sukesh-danna looked out his palace window and saw his people talking and standing idly about. He summoned his chief minister and demanded to know the reason.

"Sire," said the minister. "They speak of a distant city of marvels, a city named Uruk, whose king is Mer-kar. Around its walls are fertile lands where every sort of plant and animal thrives. Within its gates are busy streets where every sort of craft and precious good is sold. High above the city is the temple of Inanna, whose shining walls make rainbows reaching up to heaven."

When King Sukesh-danna heard this, his face grew dark and angry.

"Send forth a message," he ordered, "to that king of that city. Tell him thus: he must submit to me, for it is here in her temple of Aratta that the goddess Inanna truly dwells. He may have built her a temple of painted bricks, but I have built her a temple with real lapis lazuli. He may

3

have seen Inanna there in a dream, but I have seen her
face to face, here in Aratta."

The chief minister bowed and went to find the king's best
messenger. The lad flew over the mountains like a falcon.
He crossed the plains as fleet as a wild horse. At last he
saw the shining walls of Uruk.

The messenger came into the council chamber of King
Mer-kar, who was seated upon his throne.

"Your majesty," said the steward. "A messenger has arrived from King Sukesh-danna of Aratta."

King Mer-kar gestured to the messenger.

He bowed and said, "My lord, I bear a message from my king, Sukesh-danna of Aratta. He bids me tell you thus: you must submit to him, for it is in her temple of Aratta that the goddess Inanna truly dwells. You may have built her a temple of painted bricks, but he has built her a temple with real lapis lazuli. You may have seen Inanna here in a dream, but he has seen her face to face, there in Aratta."

The messenger arose, bowed, and awaited the reply.

The king of Uruk was silent. He motioned to his scribe for a stylus and a ball of clay. Mer-kar shaped the clay into a flat tablet and began to write upon it. When he had finished, he read it over from the beginning and rolled his royal seal across it.

One by one, his ministers took the tablet. They nodded in complete agreement with all that King Mer-kar had written.

The scribe hardened the tablet in the sun. The steward handed the tablet to the messenger. The lad departed Uruk and sped swiftly away from the City of Rainbows.

The messenger returned to the throne room of Sukesh-danna.

"Tell us," smiled the chief minister, "how the king of Uruk submitted to Aratta."

The messenger replied, "King Mer-kar made no speech, but marked upon this slab of clay."

The steward took the tablet and handed it to Sukesh-danna.

The king began to read. His face grew flushed, then pale, then dark again. He ordered everyone to leave the room. He commanded them to assemble again.

"The king of Uruk," roared Sukesh-danna, "has sent lines of warriors against me. He has turned loose hungry lions against me. He has driven wedges between me and the great goddess Inanna. How shall the king of Aratta answer?"

The ministers wrung their hands, unsure of what to advise.

"Sire," they said finally. "We wonder if perhaps, on certain occasions, when all the omens are favorable, the goddess Inanna might travel from Aratta to stay for a time in her temple that Mer-kar built at Uruk."

At this, Sukesh-danna hurled the tablet from him. It shattered into dust and fragments.

"There is my answer!" he cried. "May my city become a deserted mound of dust, my people the broken clay upon its sides. Never will Aratta submit to Uruk."

The ministers bowed low and withdrew. As they left the palace, they saw a crowd gathered in the main square. A magician was performing.

The chief minister had an idea. When the show was over, he spoke to the magician.

9

10

The minister and the magician went together into the palace. They approached the king.

"Sire," said the chief minister. "I present to you the magician Urgir-nunna. He is no ordinary magician, but a great sorcerer from the city of Hamazu, famous for its wizards."

Urgir-nunna bowed and took a special scarf and vessel from his pack. He called for water and oil. The sorcerer asked Sukesh-danna to hold the cloth before his face.

"Now unveil your eyes, O king of Aratta, and gaze into this brimming bowl of water and swirling oil."

The king saw clearly before him the rainbow walls of Uruk, surrounded by a vast army drawn from east and west, from the southern marshes to the northern mountains of the fragrant cedar. Sukesh-danna watched the people of Uruk flee their city. They were loading a few bundles on sledges, starting the long march to Aratta.

"By your magic arts," declared the king, "all this shall come to pass."

Sukesh-danna gave five minas of gold to the sorcerer and five minas of silver to the chief minister. He ordered his cooks to prepare the finest food and drink for the wizard.

Early the next morning, Urgir-nunna left Aratta for Uruk. By the end of the day, he had covered half the distance. At sunset, he entered the city of Eresh. Before him were two large barns, one for cows and the other for goats.

The sorcerer stepped inside the first barn. He bewitched the cows so they could understand and speak as people do.

13

"Cows," he said. "Who will eat your cream? Who will drink your milk?"

"The goddess Nisaba," replied the cows. "She will eat our cream and drink our milk in her temple overlooking Eresh."

14

Urgir-nunna went into the second barn. He bewitched the goats so they too could understand and speak as people do.

"Goats," he said. "Who will eat your cream? Who will drink your milk?"

"The goddess Nisaba," replied the goats. "She will eat our cream and drink our milk in her temple overlooking Eresh."

A wickedness seized the sorcerer. He cast a terrible spell over the cows and goats. Their milk dried up in an instant. The calves bawled in hunger. The kids bleated piteously. Their mothers could do nothing for them.

15

16

When the twin brothers who served the goddess Nisaba as dairymen came to fill the pails, there was not even a drop of milk. The sacred bowls and churns of Nisaba stood empty.

The dairymen had seen a stranger near their barns. The innkeeper told them the man was a sorcerer journeying to Uruk for King Sukesh-danna of Aratta.

At dawn, the brothers knelt on either side of the eastern gate of Eresh. They appealed to the sun god.

"A sorcerer journeying to Uruk for Sukesh-danna of Aratta entered our barns. He cast a terrible spell over the cows and goats. Their milk dried up in an instant. The calves bawl in hunger. The kids bleat piteously. He has dared to tamper with the cream and milk of the goddess Nisaba."

17

The sun god was much displeased. He sent a shaft of light through the window of a cottage just outside the walls of Eresh, where a woman named Sag-burru lived.

She was young in the time of the kings of long ago. She was versed in every magic art. She readied herself to meet Urgir-nunna.

The sorcerer arrived at the banks of the Euphrates, within sight of the shining walls of Uruk. Sag-burru was waiting on the opposite shore. She raised her hand in challenge.

From her cloak, she took out three wands of purest copper. Urgir-nunna reached into his pack and took out three wands of purest copper.

They threw the first wand into the river. The sorcerer pulled out a giant carp from the water. Sag-burru pulled out an eagle, which snatched the fish and flew off to its mountain nest.

They threw the second wand into the river. The sorcerer pulled out a ewe and her lamb from the water. Sag-burru pulled out a wolf, which snatched the sheep and rushed off to its rocky cave.

19

They threw the third wand into the river. The sorcerer pulled out a cow and her calf from the water. Sag-burru pulled out a lion, which snatched the kine and ran off to its thicket den.

The sorcerer knew he had lost the challenge.

"Unfortunate Urgir-nunna," said Sag-burru. "Why have you squandered your skills? Why did you bring your wizard's ways to my city of Eresh?"

The sorcerer humbly bent his head. "Worthy Sag-burru, I erred in doing magic in your city. I neglected to accord proper respect to you. Let me return to Aratta, where I will make known your greatness in all the lands."

"Miserable Urgir-nunna," continued Sag-burru. "Why did you cause the calf and kid to suffer? Why did you dare tamper with the holy cream and milk of Nisaba? The gods cannot forgive your deed."

Sag-burru pronounced ancient, powerful words, and the sorcerer ceased to live. She removed the core of magic from his body. The milk flowed again in the barns of Nisaba.

When Sukesh-danna learned what had befallen the sorcerer, he saw that the gods had revealed their wishes. To Mer-kar, King of Uruk, he sent this message: "You are the chosen one of the great goddess Inanna. I must submit to you, for it is in the City of Rainbows that Inanna truly dwells."

Notes to the Story

The ancient land of **Sumer** was in southern Mesopotamia (modern Iraq) between the Tigris and Euphrates Rivers. There, **Uruk** and its neighboring cities flourished, especially during the third millennium B.C. While many of these cities were politically independent, with their own kings and royal courts, they shared a common Sumerian culture, religion, language, and literature.

The patron deity of Uruk was **Inanna**, the principal goddess of the Sumerian pantheon. On a high platform overlooking the city sat her temple, its walls and columns inlaid with gleaming bricks: **the rainbow walls of Uruk.**

Uruk's most famous king was Gilgamesh, whose legendary exploits are recounted in *The Epic of Gilgamesh,* the best-known work of Mesopotamian literature. About 2700 B.C., **Mer-kar**, one of Gilgamesh's royal ancestors, ruled Uruk, a sage and benevolent king credited with great building projects. Five hundred years after Mer-kar's death, *The City of Rainbows* was composed, part of a series of tales in which the wise King Mer-kar triumphs over the foolish King **Sukesh-danna** of **Aratta**, a city far from Sumer.

Though the precise location of Aratta is unknown, the city was in Elam (modern Iran), probably on a trade route linking Mesopotamia with the **lapis lazuli** quarries further east in Afghanistan. Throughout the ancient world, lapis lazuli stones were costly treasures, much prized for their deep blue color.

The Sumerians regarded other peoples as culturally inferior, particularly because they were ignorant of the Sumerian invention of writing. Mer-kar responds to Sukesh-danna's long-winded demand by calling for tablet clay and a cut reed **stylus**. He writes an answer, presumably barbed and clever. Then he signs it with a roll of his **royal seal**, a small cylinder engraved with his personal design of miniature figures, such as lions, heroes, and gods.

When the baffled messenger returns with Mer-kar's silent reply, not even the king is able to read the tablet. Sukesh-danna sees the lines of writing as rows of warriors marching against him; the figures of Mer-kar's seal as lions ready to devour him; and the triangular marks made by the stylus as wedges driven between himself and the goddess Inanna.

Sukesh-danna turns to omens and magic as a way out of his predicament. For guidance, Mesopotamians often consulted specialists who foretold the future by observing such omens as the flight of birds, the shape of clouds, and the swirling rainbows of oil in water. Sukesh-danna rewards the sorcerer **Urgir-nunna** for seeing a satisfactory omen by giving the magician five **minas** of gold, about two and one-half kilos.

Eresh, where Urgir-nunna stops on his way to Uruk, was a small city in the outlying districts of Sumer. **Nisaba** was its patron deity, a goddess of grain and scribal arts. Like other Mesopotamian deities, she received daily offerings of food and drink in her temple, with sacred animals kept for that purpose. Urgir-nunna's wickedness in tampering with the goddess Nisaba's milk supply was an affront to the gods, as well as to **Sag-burru**, the resident sorceress of Eresh.

Within sight of the rainbow walls of Uruk, Urgir-nunna loses three transformation challenges to Sag-burru. The magician must die. Sag-burru lifts the spell cast over Nisaba's cows and goats by removing the **core of magic** from the dead sorcerer. This may have been his tongue, which the Mesopotamians considered a prime source of power, for good or evil.

King Sukesh-danna yields to Mer-kar, King of Uruk, as every Sumerian audience knew he would. *The City of Rainbows* ends happily.

23

Mesopotamian Writing and Literature

Mesopotamian writing, invented in Sumer before 3000 B.C., was done by impressing cut reeds into soft clay tablets, creating the script known today as cuneiform (Latin for wedge-shaped). Thousands of Sumerian documents have survived, treating every aspect of daily life. Among the most interesting tablets are those with the world's oldest stories, epics, myths, and poetry. Many works of literature remained popular for centuries, and were recopied in Akkadian, the language that eventually replaced Sumerian throughout Mesopotamia.

In retelling the story I have titled *The City of Rainbows*, I have relied on Adele Berlin's *Enmerkar and Ensuḫkeśdanna: A Sumerian Narrative Poem* (Philadelphia: The University Museum, 1979). This is a scholarly publication of the thirty-three tablets preserving different portions of the tale, from which Berlin assembled a composite text. *The City of Rainbows* presents typical editing problems, in that sections are missing and parts of lines are broken away. I have followed the Sumerian original as closely as possible. In some places, I have filled in gaps or reworked obscure passages, guided by other Mesopotamian writings and art and archaeological material.

As seen here, a common feature of Mesopotamian literature is repetition, a device in which speeches, descriptions, and events are repeated two or three times in the story. This helped Mesopotamian listeners at literary recitations remember what had already occurred in the narrative.

About the Illustrations

Mesopotamian literature was not illustrated, though occasionally scenes from mythology appear on cylinder seals. In fitting images to the characters and events of this tale, I have created cut-paper compositions based on actual Sumerian mosaics made of pieces of lapis lazuli, shell, and red limestone set into bitumen, a sticky black substance. These were widely used to decorate furniture, small boxes, and musical instruments, as well as temple and palace walls. The mosaics chosen for *The City of Rainbows* come from Tell Ubaid, Mari, Telloh, and the Royal Graves at Ur.

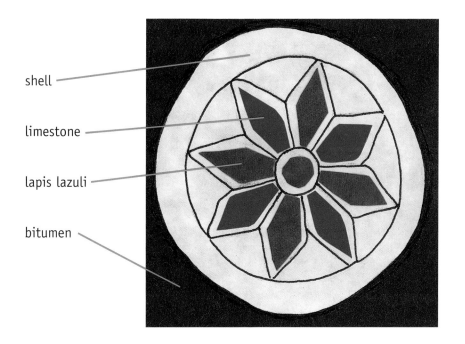

shell

limestone

lapis lazuli

bitumen

An Original Tablet of *The City of Rainbows*

About 1750 B.C., a schoolboy or his teacher at Nippur, a city near Uruk, copied out part of *The City of Rainbows* on this 12 x 7 cm clay tablet. The schoolroom, where many other tablets were found by modern archaeologists, was located in a private house. Sitting on built-in benches, beginning students mixed clay and practiced elementary cuneiform signs. More advanced pupils studied literature by copying texts over and over until the teacher was satisfied. This neatly made tablet, with its carefully written signs, may be the work of a young man nearly ready to be a scribe, or the schoolmaster's own model text.

The first twelve lines of this tablet conclude the episode in which King Sukesh-danna tries to conceal from his ministers that he cannot read King Mer-kar's message. For a Sumerian boy learning to be a scribe, this must have been a favorite scene. In the tablet's last six lines, the sorcerer enters the tale. Today, this tablet is in the Babylonian Section of the University of Pennsylvania Museum of Archaeology and Anthropology.

26

For Further Reading

Crawford, Harriet. *Sumer and the Sumerians*. Cambridge: Cambridge University Press, 1991.

Foster, Benjamin R. *From Distant Days: Myths, Tales, and Poetry of Ancient Mesopotamia*. Bethesda, MD: CDL Press, 1995.

Kovacs, Maureen Gallery. *The Epic of Gilgamesh*. Stanford: Stanford University Press, 1989.

Kramer, Samuel Noah. *History Begins at Sumer*. Philadelphia: University of Pennsylvania Press, 1981.

McCall, Henrietta. *Mesopotamian Myths*. London: British Museum Press, 1990.

Oppenheim, A. Leo. *Ancient Mesopotamia: Portrait of a Dead Civilization*. Chicago: University of Chicago Press, 1977.

Roaf, Michael. *Cultural Atlas of Mesopotamia and the Ancient Near East*. Oxford: Facts on File, 1990.

Walker, C. B. F. *Cuneiform*. London: British Museum Press, 1987.